ICE AGE™
DAWN OF THE DINOSAURS

THE JUNIOR NOVEL

Library of Congress catalog card number: 2008942545
ISBN 978-0-06-168980-2
09 10 11 12 13   LP/CW/UG   10 9 8 7 6 5 4 3 2 1
❖
First Edition

ICE AGE™
DAWN OF THE DINOSAURS

THE JUNIOR NOVEL

ADAPTED BY SUSAN KORMAN

HARPER

ENTERTAINMENT

An Imprint of HarperCollinsPublishers

ICE AGE™
DAWN OF THE DINOSAURS

THE JUNIOR NOVEL

CHAPTER
ONE

"**B**e careful, guys!" Manny warned the possums. "I need that!"

Crash and Eddie nodded and then turned back to gaze at the sparkling ice crystal that hung from a snow-covered tree branch. A tunnel of thick, protective webbing surrounded it. The possum brothers bumped fists and began moving through the maze of threads like soldiers on a mission.

Crash dipped under one sticky web and then carefully curved his tail over another. The crystal was closer now. He leaped up to grab a branch, but the bark peeled off in his hands. He screamed as he plummeted downward.

Eddie reached out and grabbed him in the nick of time. "Are you hit?" he asked.

"Negatory," Crash replied.

Manny rolled his eyes. "Would you two just get the crystal?" he snapped.

The possums flipped and twisted their way through the web toward the gleaming sparkler. At last, Crash plucked the precious object from its base. "Got it!" he declared triumphantly.

"Good." Manny heaved a sigh of relief. "Now get it down here."

Crash started down the spiderweb. But the tip of the crystal suddenly nicked a silky strand. A vibration rippled through the web.

"Uh-oh," Eddie said in a panic.

"Get out of there!" yelled Manny. "Now!"

Crash and Eddie held the crystal over their heads, racing through the spiderweb tunnel.

"Go! Go! Go!" Crash cried.

Eight glowing eyes suddenly appeared in the darkness. It was the spider! Moving with lightning speed, the spider took off after the possums.

Crash and Eddie raced on through the web—until they got caught on a twig! The twig snapped, sending the possums flying from the tunnel. The crystal sailed into the air, landing right in Sid's hands.

The furious spider dropped down in front of the sloth, her eyes blazing. Sid screamed, frantically tossing the crystal away as if it were a hot potato.

Manny dived—and caught it.

Relieved, the woolly mammoth held the crystal close to his face. "This is it," he murmured, "the finishing touch for my project."

He ran off with the prize, and the possums followed.

CHAPTER
TWO

Later that day, Manny led his mate, Ellie, through the woods, their friends trailing along behind them. Manny had covered Ellie's eyes with his trunk; he had a special surprise to show her.

"Alright, it's not ready yet, but . . . *voilà!*" he pronounced dramatically, uncovering her eyes.

Ellie let out a startled gasp. She was standing in the middle of a spectacular playground. It had a seesaw, swings made from vines, an obstacle course, even a circular ice slide.

She was so stunned, she could barely speak.

"I made it myself. It's for our baby," Manny said proudly.

"It's amazing, Manny," Ellie said. Just then, a sparkling object caught her eye. An ice mobile decorated with a large glittering crystal dangled from a tree branch. It held three tiny carved figures—Ellie, Manny, and a baby woolly mammoth.

"Oh, Manny," Ellie murmured, touched. "How beautiful."

Manny beamed. "I made that, too. It's our family."

"Hey, Manny." Sid gazed up at the mobile with a frown. "How come I'm not up there?"

"You can be on *our* mobile," Eddie offered.

Giggling, Crash held up a mobile made of live spiders and creepy dead things.

"Of course I'd never let the baby in here

like this! Sharp corners, choking rocks—and can you imagine the germ count? It's basically a death trap!"

Ellie watched him, shaking her head. "You're trying to baby-proof nature, Manny," she said. "Our baby is going to grow up in this world. You can't change that."

"Of course I can," Manny argued, puffing up his chest. "I'm a woolly mammoth—the biggest thing on Earth!"

"All right, Mr. Big Stuff," Ellie shot back, teasing him. "But when—" Suddenly, she winced.

"What?" Manny cried. "Is it happening? You're going into labor! Take a deep breath!"

"Manny!" Ellie said. "It was just a kick." She reached over and grabbed his trunk. Tenderly, she held it to her belly.

Manny smiled happily as he felt the

baby squirm inside her.

Ellie turned back to her husband. "Manny, I know you're excited. I am, too. But you're getting a little carried away."

"You're starting to sound like Diego," Manny teased. "Wait," he added. "Where's Diego?"

Manny shrugged. "I haven't seen him for a while."

"That's odd," Ellie murmured. She hadn't seen the saber-toothed tiger today, either.

Soon it was time to head back home. Manny was about to close the playground gate when he spotted Sid. The sloth was still inside, reaching toward a snow sculpture.

"I don't want you touching anything," Manny warned him. "This place is for kids. Are you a kid?"

Sid was about to reply when Manny spoke up again. "On second thought, don't answer that."

Sid touched the snow sculpture anyway, breaking off its head.

But before Manny could scold him again, a deflated Diego approached. Having just lost chase to a gazelle, he'd just realized he was no longer the fit feline he used to be.

"Diego, there you are!" Manny said. "You missed the big surprise."

"Oh, right." Diego looked away. "I'll check it out later."

"Okay, see you then," Manny replied nonchalantly.

Huh? Ellie thought, watching them. Diego and Manny were best friends. What in the world was going on between the two of them?

CHAPTER THREE

As the saber walked away, Ellie turned to Manny. "I think there's something bothering Diego," she said.

Manny shook his head. "Everything's fine," he replied.

"You should go talk to him," Ellie urged him.

"Guys don't *talk* to guys about guy problems," Manny reminded her. "We just punch each other on the shoulder. Like this." He balled his trunk into a fist and punched her lightly.

Ellie gave him a stern look. "That's stupid."

"Okay, okay." Manny relented. "I'm going."

Diego stood staring out at the tundra.

Manny walked over and punched him on the shoulder.

"Ow!" Diego said. "Why'd you do that?" he demanded.

Manny shrugged. "I don't know . . ." There was an awkward silence, and then Manny blurted out, "Ellie thinks there's something bothering you. But I told her—"

"Actually," Diego cut in, "I've been thinking that, maybe soon, it might be time for me to head out. . . . You know, on my own."

Manny blinked, and then patted his friend. "Okay. So I'll tell her you're fine, it was nothing, and—"

"Look, Manny, who are we kidding?" Diego tried again. "I'm not a kitty cat. I'm a saber-toothed tiger. I'm not built for chaperoning playdates."

Manny was bewildered. "What are you talking about?" he asked.

"Having a family, that's huge. And I'm happy for you and all, but . . . but . . ."

Diego's words trailed off. "But that's your adventure," he finished. "Not mine."

"You don't want to be around my kid?" Manny was hurt. "Is that what you're saying?"

"No, no, no." Diego shook his head. "You're taking this the wrong way."

"Well, go find some adventure, Mr. Adventure Guy!" Manny snapped. "Don't let my domestic life slow you down!"

With that, Manny stalked back toward Ellie. "See, that's why guys don't talk to guys!"

"Why? What happened?" Ellie asked, concerned.

"Diego's leaving," Manny informed her.

Sid had been listening to the whole exchange. "Whoa, whoa, whoa!" he said. "Nobody has to go anywhere. This should be the best time of our lives. We're having a baby!"

"No, Sid," Diego snapped. *"They're having a baby."*

"But we're a herd," Sid reminded him. "A family!"

"Look." Diego's voice was hard. "Things have changed. Manny has other priorities now."

Sid slumped.

"Face it, Sid," Diego added in a gentler tone. "We had a great run together. But now it's time to move on."

Sid looked at him. "So you mean it's just the two of us now?"

Diego shook his head. "It's not just the two of us."

"Crash and Eddie are coming, too?" Sid asked hopefully.

Diego shook his head again.

Sid stared at him, the terrible truth sinking in.

"Bye, Sid," Diego said.

The sloth watched in dismay as Diego headed one way while Manny and Ellie walked together in the opposite direction.

CHAPTER FOUR

Sid trudged alone through the frozen tundra. His whole world was crumbling.

"Calm down," he told himself. "Things will work out. I'll make my own herd."

"Hey!" he called to some nearby animals. "*¡Mis amigos! ¿Qué pasa?* What's happening, my friends?"

Instantly, the birds flapped and glyptodons disappeared inside their armored shells.

Sid sighed. So far it didn't look like anybody wanted to be in his new herd.

The sloth stared down at his reflection in the ice. "Oh, well," he told himself. "At least you've still got your looks."

Crack!

Just then, the ice under his feet gave way.

Before he knew what was happening, Sid found himself falling through the frozen ground, dropping down into a strange underground chamber.

"Oh, great," he muttered, gazing around. "Where am I?"

"Anybody here?" Sid called out. "Anyone?"

Cautiously, he stepped toward a shaft of light up ahead and then walked through the archway he saw.

Sid blinked in surprise. Sitting right in front of him were three enormous, perfectly shaped eggs.

"Oh, wow," the sloth said in awe. He looked around again, wondering about their mother.

"Hello?" Sid's voice echoed through the

empty chamber. He inched closer to the eggs.

"Poor guys," he murmured. "I know what it's like to be abandoned by your family."

Gently, he brushed dirt off the eggs. "Don't worry," he said tenderly. "You're not alone anymore."

Sid managed to lift the eggs from the chamber. Outside on the frozen tundra, he tried different ways to carry them. Finally, he gave up and began rolling the gigantic eggs along the ground, one at a time.

The lazy sloth wasn't used to working this hard. A few minutes later, he had to sit down to take a break. "Whew!" he said. "This is exhausting!"

Just then, one of the eggs rolled past. It bumped across the ice and sailed down a hill.

Sid screamed. "Stay here," he ordered

the other two eggs. Then he took off after the one careening down the hill. "Momma's coming, baby!" he yelled frantically. "Momma's coming!"

Sid leaped through the air to stop the egg. "Gotcha," he said in relief.

Thump. Thump.

The other two eggs rolled past him. "What did I just tell you kids?" Sid cried.

He positioned himself in front of one egg to stop it. But the egg bowled him over instead, sending him flying onto some bark lying nearby.

Sid managed to steer the bark like a sled and grab hold of two of the eggs. He clung to them as he sped after the last egg. Just as he reached it, the sled hit something and launched into the air. Sid and the eggs flew off.

Sid grabbed two of the eggs in midair.

Desperately, he reached for the third one with his feet. But as he landed on a ledge, the egg slipped from his grasp.

"Oh, no!" Sid gasped. The egg plummeted below, heading straight for a row of jagged rocks!

CHAPTER FIVE

"**W**hat's that?" Ellie murmured to Manny. A large, oval-shaped object was flying toward them. She reached out with her trunk and snatched it.

"Thank you! Thank you!" Sid cried, rushing toward them. Then he scowled at the runaway egg. "Bad egg!" he scolded it. "Rotten egg! You almost gave me a heart attack!"

He took the egg from Ellie and hugged it tightly. "I'm sorry, darling," he said. "It's just that I love you so much! Now I want you to meet your uncle Manny and aunt Ellie."

Sid presented the eggs to his friends, one at a time. "I'd like you to meet Egbert, Shelly, and Yoko."

Ellie waved, amused to see that Sid had actually drawn smiley faces on the shells.

But Manny frowned. "Sid, whatever you're doing, it's a bad idea," he said.

"*Shhh!*" Sid hushed Manny, putting his hands on one of the eggs, as if it had ears. "My kids will hear you."

"They're not your kids, Sid!" Manny snapped. "Take them back. You're not meant to be a parent."

"Why not?" Sid demanded.

"The first sign?" Manny began. "You stole someone else's eggs. The second sign? One of your 'babies' almost became an omelet!"

"Someone's probably looking for them, worried sick," Ellie added.

"No!" Sid shook his head vehemently. "They were underground in ice. If it weren't for me, they'd be frozen *eggsicles*."

Manny softened. "Sid," he tried again, "I know what you're going through. Trust me, you'll have a family, too, someday. You'll meet a nice girl. Someone who . . . someone who . . ." He looked at his friend and then blurted out, "Well, someone who has no real options—or sense of smell."

"Sid," Ellie jumped in. "What Manny means to say is—"

"Oh, I get it," Sid cut her off. "I'll take them back. You can have your family, but I'm better off alone."

Nearby he found a hollowed-out log to use as a stroller. "I'll be a fortress of solitude in the ice, alone forever," he muttered. "A lone, lonely loner." With that, he disappeared around a corner.

"That's a lot of aloneness," Manny commented.

"Precisely!" Sid shot back.

Ellie looked at Manny, upset. Another one of their friends had just left the herd.

Sid marched across the snowy ground, pushing the eggs.

"Why should I take you back?" he said bitterly. "I love kids. I'm responsible, loving, and nurturing. Don't you agree?" he asked the eggs.

There was no response.

"I knew you would agree with me," Sid said.

A few minutes later, it started to rain. The faces he'd drawn on the eggs began to smear.

"Don't cry," Sid said. "Whatever you do, don't cry. I'll find a dry place." He pulled the eggs under a rock ledge. "Here, let me dry you off." As he tried to clean up the eggs, he just smeared their faces even more. He realized he was exhausted.

"Boy, parenting is a lot of work," he said aloud. "Maybe Manny was right. Maybe I'm *not* ready to be a parent."

But at that moment, something amazing happened. The sun came back out, lighting up the eggs so that Sid could make out the tiny baby silhouettes inside.

"Oh . . . wow . . . ," Sid whispered in awe. Then he leaned closer, cuddling the eggs tenderly.

CHAPTER
SIX

The next morning, Sid yawned and then rolled off the rock where he slept. He was still half asleep as he shuffled through his dimly lit cave.

Suddenly, he realized that someone was following him. He whirled around and spotted three baby . . .

"Dinosaurs!" he gasped.

"Momma!" they squealed, rushing over to him.

Sid was filled with happiness. "I'm a mommy!" he declared, hugging the dinosaurs tightly. He'd finally found a new herd.

• • •

Sid and the kids were playing in the woods later that day when they spotted something—Manny's playground. The three of them gazed at it longingly from behind the fence.

"No." Sid shook his head firmly. "I'm sorry, but you can't go in. Manny says it's just for kids."

The dinosaurs whimpered, their eyes pleading with him.

"Wait a minute!" Sid realized. "You are kids." He reached over and unlatched the gate. "Okay," he said, giving in. "Just don't break anything."

The dinos bounded inside.

An aardvark shovel-mouth boy had been watching the whole scene. When he saw the dinosaurs entering the playground, he opened up his big mouth and shouted, "The sloth says the playground is open!"

"No! Wait!" Sid cried in a panic. "It's not open for *everyone*!"

But it was too late. Kids poured into the playground from every direction, stampeding Sid.

The sloth raced around, desperately trying to manage the situation.

"No, no, no!" he screamed. "Don't touch that!" He rushed over to rescue some kids who were stuck on one end of the seesaw because a baby dinosaur held down the other end. Another baby dinosaur whipped past, with a beaver kid hanging from his tail.

A mole-hog mom stared curiously at the young dinosaurs. "What are they?" she asked.

"Who cares?" answered the beaver kid. "They're fun!"

"Play nice!" Sid kept calling to the

three dinosaurs.

"Mommy!" A beaver girl yelled suddenly. "He's not sharing!"

Sid looked over. Baby Dinosaur Three was fighting with the beaver girl over a stick.

The beaver mom looked at Sid. "Aren't you going to do something?" she demanded.

Sid narrowed his eyes at her. "Like what? My kid had it first."

"Did not!" snapped the beaver girl.

"Did too!" Sid shot back.

"Did not!" she repeated.

"Liar, liar, fur on fire!" shouted Sid.

The beaver mother was appalled. "What's the matter with you?" she asked Sid.

"I'm a single mother with three kids!" he snapped back. "I could use a little compassion!"

"Slow down! Please, slow down!" a mole-hog kid yelled.

Sid turned to see Baby Dinosaur Two spinning kids around and around inside the turtle shell. The shell was spinning so fast, it was a blur of motion.

"Look out!" Sid yelled.

But it was too late. The kids shot into the air, rocketing across the playground.

Meanwhile, Baby Dinosaur One was pushing the shovel-mouth boy way too high on the vine swings.

"Stop! Stop! Stop!" cried the boy.

His mother watched, frantic. "Ronald!" she yelled helplessly.

Just then, Baby Dinosaur One shoved Ronald hard—so hard the boy flew into the air and out of the playground.

"Oh, boy," Sid mumbled. "That's a shame."

Things only got worse. On the circular slide, an aardvark boy held on desperately to the top while Baby Dinosaur Two pushed him from behind. Baby Dinosaur Three waited at the bottom, his mouth open wide and his sharp teeth flashing.

"No!" the aardvark boy shouted. "No!"

"Hold on, little Johnny!" his mother screamed.

"I'm trying!" he yelled back.

At that, Baby Dinosaur Two shoved him, and little Johnny began circling down the slide, screaming all the way.

When the aardvark reached the bottom, he slid right into Baby Dinosaur Three's mouth. The dinosaur swallowed him up.

Sid turned to the other mothers. "You know," he remarked, "experts say you should let your kids eat whatever they want to eat."

The mothers screamed loudly. Then they frantically scooped up their children and rushed from the playground.

CHAPTER
SEVEN

Manny and Ellie were walking through the woods with the possums when a loud scream rang out. A shovel-mouth boy came hurtling toward them. Manny flung out his trunk, catching him like a fly ball.

"Ronald?" Manny knew the boy. "Where did you come from?"

The shovel-mouth boy pointed behind them.

"Oh, no!" Manny gasped. The playground—the beautiful playground he'd lovingly built for his baby—was filled with screaming kids and parents.

Inside, Sid marched over to Baby Dinosaur Three, who had his mouth clenched shut.

"Come on, spit him out!" Sid said sternly.

Baby Dinosaur Three shook his head no.

"If you don't spit out little Johnny," Sid went on, "we're leaving the playground this instant." He began counting. "One . . ."

The dinosaur let out a whimper.

"Two . . ." Sid glared at him. "Don't make me say three . . ."

Finally, Baby Dinosaur Three opened his mouth—and spat out a wet and dazed-looking little bird.

Sid turned to Johnny's mother. "There we are," he said triumphantly. "He's fine— the picture of health."

"That's not little Johnny!" she exclaimed, staring in horror at the bird.

Sid shrugged. "It's better than nothing." Then he leaned over and nudged Baby Dinosaur Three. "Come on, barf him up."

Baby Dinosaur Three spat out the aardvark boy. Little Johnny was crying and covered with slime.

"Sid!" someone shouted.

Sid gulped when he saw Manny and Ellie marching toward him. "Oh, hey," he called nervously. "Hey, Manny!"

The mother aardvark scooped up her little boy and scurried away. As they rushed past, Baby Dinosaur Three leaned over to give Johnny one last lick. Then the dinosaur began backing away.

"Wait!" Manny cried.

But it was too late. As the dinosaur stepped backward, his head crashed into the ice mobile that Manny had made. It fell, shattering into pieces as it hit the ground.

For a moment, no one moved or said a word. Then Manny bent down and began sifting through the broken shards with his trunk.

Sid approached him, hanging his head. "I'm really sorry, Manny," he said sheepishly.

Manny ignored Sid, his eyes still taking in the terrible damage all around.

"This place is totaled," Crash muttered under his breath.

"And we didn't wreck it," Eddie added.

"We're losing our edge, bro," said Crash.

"The important thing is that no one got hurt," Sid blurted out. "Except for that guy." He pointed to an injured animal. "And, well, those three. Oh, and that girl, too. . . ."

Manny wheeled toward Sid, furious.

"I told you to take those eggs back!" he snarled. "But you kept them! And now look what they've done!"

Sid stepped backward. "Okay," he agreed. "Granted, we do have some discipline issues here, but—"

Manny cut him off again. "Eating kids is not a discipline issue!"

"But he spit them out!" Sid pointed out.

"Well, that's super," Manny retorted. "Let's give him a gold star. He's kid of the week." He leaned in closer to Sid. "They don't belong here, Sid. Whatever they are, wherever you found them, take them back!"

"Manny?" Sid swallowed hard. "I am not getting rid of my kids."

Suddenly, the earth below their feet rumbled. Overhead, birds darted from tree to tree, frantically searching for safety.

Uh-oh, Ellie thought, watching a terrified bird—a huge diatryma—sink her head into the ground. It's an earthquake!

CHAPTER EIGHT

The baby dinosaurs clung to Sid as the earth continued to tremble.

"It's okay." Sid tried to calm them down. "Momma's here."

The animals looked around anxiously.

BOOM!

The earth gave a sudden, violent jolt. Then there was a loud, strange-sounding shriek.

Terrified, the possums jumped up onto Ellie's tusks.

"Do earthquakes shriek?" Crash wanted to know.

BOOM! BOOM!

A long shadow unrolled along the

ground. Ellie looked up and felt her jaw drop open. Towering over them was an enormous dinosaur!

"I thought those guys were extinct!" Ellie said.

"Then that is one angry fossil!" Manny said, eyeing the ferocious-looking beast. "I have a feeling she's looking for her babies. SID!" he screamed.

The sloth was desperately herding the baby dinosaurs into a cave. "Come on," he urged them. "Come on. Inside, inside, inside!"

The mother dinosaur sniffed the ground. Then she let out another huge roar that echoed through the valley.

Animals scrambled in every direction, trying to escape.

"Nobody move a muscle," Manny called, as the dinosaur scanned the area.

Sid huddled with the dinosaurs inside the cave. By now they were all wailing loudly.

"No. *Shhh*," Sid said. "Don't cry. Don't cry." He began singing a lullaby.

The reptiles only sobbed louder.

BOOM! BOOM!

Sid stopped singing as the footsteps came closer . . . and closer. . . . All at once they stopped.

RIIIPP!

With one swift motion, the mother dinosaur tore off the top of the cave and tossed it aside. Terrified, Sid jumped into the dinosaurs' arms.

Manny and Ellie were hiding behind a rock.

"Sid!" Manny screamed. "Give them to her! She's their mother!"

"How do I *know* she's their mother?"

Sid yelled back.

"Do you want a birth certificate?" Manny shouted. "She's a dinosaur. Of course she's their mother!"

"But I put in the blood, sweat, and tears to raise them!" Sid sobbed.

"For a day!" Manny yelled. "Give them back, you lunatic!"

Bravely, Sid stood in front of the mother dinosaur. "Look, Momma!" he said fiercely. "These are *my* kids, and you're going to have to go through me to get them."

The mother dinosaur cocked her head, as if she were thinking.

Sid held his breath. *Maybe she'll give up and go away,* he thought.

Instead, Momma leaned forward. With one swift motion, she snatched up her kids—and Sid!

BOOM! BOOM! BOOM!

The ground thundered as the dinosaur

turned and marched away.

"Sid!" Ellie screamed.

"Sid!" cried Manny.

They raced after him.

After leaving Manny and Ellie, Diego had roamed far from the village. He was chasing a gazelle out on the plains when he heard an unusual cry.

Roar!

Diego froze in his tracks. The ground under his feet rumbled as an enormous creature charged across the plains.

That's a dinosaur! Diego realized in surprise. As he stared in disbelief, he saw that she was holding something in her mouth—three little dinosaurs and a . . .

Sloth? Diego thought. *Could it be? Was it really . . . ?*

"Help!" Sid screamed at the top of his lungs. "Somebody help me!"

CHAPTER NINE

"**S**id must be down there," Manny said. He stood with Ellie and the possums, peering down into a massive hole in the ground. Jagged slabs of earth framed a rocky path that sloped off into the darkness. Wisps of steam rose up ominously.

Crash and Eddie gulped.

"He's dead by now," Eddie said.

"It's a real shame," Crash added solemnly. "He'll be missed."

Together the possums bowed their heads. Then they tried to slip away.

"Oh, no you don't." Ellie blocked their path with her trunk. "Not so fast, you two."

Manny looked at her, worried. "This is where I draw the line, Ellie. You, Crash, and Eddie need to go back to the village. Now."

"Yeah, that's going to happen," Ellie said sarcastically. She brushed past Manny and entered the hole.

"But, Ellie, wait!" Manny called. "You saw that dinosaur. This is going to be dangerous."

"Talk to the trunk," Ellie called back.

With a sigh Manny started after her. "After we save Sid, I'm going to kill him," he muttered.

Crash and Eddie stood at the edge of the hole, still hesitating.

"Ladies first," Crash said to Eddie.

"Age before beauty," Eddie replied.

"No pain, no gain," Crash said next.

Eddie squinted at him. "What pain?" he asked.

At that, Crash pushed Eddie into the hole. Crash started laughing—until he realized that Eddie had hooked his tail around Crash's neck. Together they tumbled downward.

The friends soon found themselves in an eerie cavernous world. Ice shards reflected lava's flickering glow, and large dinosaur skulls and bones littered the ground.

"Sid?" Everyone called together. "Sid?"

Manny came up to Ellie. "Stay close to me," he told her, glancing around uneasily. Manny jumped as a figure suddenly lunged out of the darkness.

"Diego?" Manny's mouth dropped open in surprise. "What in the world are you doing down here?"

"Vacationing," Diego replied sarcastically. "I'm looking for Sid, the same as you," he added a second later.

Manny opened his mouth, about to make a wisecrack, but Ellie cut him off.

"Great!" she said warmly. "We need all the help we can get."

Suddenly, a large spiked tail slammed down in front of them. Ellie jumped—it belonged to an angry-looking ankylosaurus.

The dinosaur crashed its tail into some rocks, sending debris everywhere and nearly crushing Diego.

Diego jumped back. "Never mind!" he said.

The ankylosaurus loomed over them, its jaws snapping. The creature was about to devour them all at once, when Ellie spotted another huge dinosaur. It was a diplodocus munching on some tree leaves.

Thinking fast, she ripped a green frond from a plant and shook it over the edge of the cliff where they stood.

"Here, boy!" she shouted, as if she were calling a dog. "Here!"

Sure enough, the long-necked diplodocus turned in her direction. When he saw the juicy-looking frond, he came over and began munching on it.

"Climb on!" Ellie urged everyone. "Get onto his back!"

"We're not getting on that thing!" Manny declared.

"It's this dinosaur or . . ." Ellie pointed to the mean-looking ankylosaurus who was still eyeing them hungrily. "Or that one!"

With that, she and the possums jumped onto the diplodocus's head. Manny and Diego hesitated for one more second. But just as the ankylosaurus came closer, they jumped aboard, too.

The diplodocus lifted his head high over the view, away from the ankylosaurus.

A few minutes later, the friends slid down the creature's tail, landing in a pile on the ground.

Whew, Manny thought in relief. *We're safe.*

But when he looked up again, he saw dozens of scary-looking beasts towering over them!

CHAPTER
TEN

Manny stood frozen, staring in terror at the enormous dinosaurs.

All of a sudden, loud trumpeting rang out.

Manny's mouth dropped open as a weasel swung on a vine in front of them.

"Take cover!" the weasel yelled. He yanked some fruit from his belt and tossed it onto the ground. A thick cloud of smoke instantly surrounded Manny and the others.

"Come on!" Using the smoke as a screen, the weasel led them away from the dinosaurs into a dense jungle.

As they walked along, the weasel expertly scanned the area for more dangers.

Crash and Eddie watched in awe.

"Dude!" Crash gushed. "You're awesome! You're like the brother I never had."

"The name's Buck," the weasel declared. "Short for Buckminster." He stared at them. "What are you doing here?"

"Our friend was taken by a dinosaur," Ellie explained.

"Well, he's dead," Buck replied. "Welcome to my world. Now, go home."

Manny glanced at Ellie. She was holding her ground.

"We're not going anywhere without Sid," she said firmly.

"Wait, Ellie," Manny said. "Maybe this deranged hermit has a point."

"We came this far, Manny," Ellie said. "We're going to find him."

Diego had wandered ahead. "I got tracks!" he called to the others.

He pointed to a set of gigantic footprints that led off the trail into the dense jungle foliage.

"If you go in there, you'll find your friend . . ." Buck's words trailed off ominously. "In the afterlife," he finished.

Crash turned to look at him. "How do you know, O great and wise weaselly one?"

Buck pointed to the tracks. "She's going to Lava Falls," he said. "It's thick jungle— where the dinos care for their newborns."

The others just stared at him.

"To get there, you've got to go through the Jungle of Misery, across the Chasm of Death, to the Plains of Woe," Buck went on.

"Woah," gasped Crash and Eddie.

Ellie swallowed hard.

Buck suddenly spun toward a nearby plant, lowering his ear as if it had said something to him.

"What?" Buck murmured. He listened for a second, and then shook his head. "No," he said. "The pterodactyls will eat them. My bet is on that."

He listened again. "The mammoth?"

They all turned to look at Manny.

Buck squinted at him as he continued talking to the plant. "Yeah, he's a fat one," he said. "They'll eat him first."

"I'm not fat!" Manny protested. "It's my fur. It's poofy."

"Manny," Diego reminded him. "You can't take this guy seriously—he's talking to a plant!"

Ellie had made up her mind. "We're going," she said firmly.

"Yeah," Manny said to Buck, as the weasel eyed the plant. "We'll leave you two to talk."

They turned to enter the jungle.

Before Manny could catch up with Ellie, Buck jumped in front of him.

"Whoa, whoa, whoa!" the weasel said. "Do you think this is some tropical getaway? You can't protect your mate here," he whispered. "And what are you going to do with those flimsy tusks of yours when you run into the *beast*?"

"The beast?" Manny echoed.

Buck nodded solemnly. "I call him . . . RUDY!"

"There's a beast?" Eddie said, quaking in fear.

"Aye." Buck nodded. "He's the one who gave me this." He pointed to the eye patch covering one eye.

"Cool!" Crash exclaimed. "He gave you that patch—*for free*?"

Buck frowned and glanced at Manny,

wondering if the possum was serious.

The mammoth patted him on the shoulder. "Welcome to my world," he said. Then he pushed Buck aside and stepped forward again.

Buck watched them all go. "Abandon all hope; he who enters there."

CHAPTER
ELEVEN

The group trekked through the thick jungle, following the mother dinosaur's prints. Soon they stepped out of the dense foliage into a lush field filled with brightly colored tropical plants.

Ellie stopped to catch her breath. "Hold on," she called.

"What's wrong?" Manny asked, worried about her again.

Ellie looked around. "I've got a funny feeling."

"You're hungry!" Manny declared. "Your blood sugar is low." He had an idea. "There's some fruit back there." He dashed toward a bush.

"No, Manny," Ellie tried to tell him. "It's not . . ."

"Wait, Manny." Diego felt uneasy, too. "I wouldn't do that if I were you. That weasel warned us about the trail; this isn't exactly your playground."

Manny snorted. "Like I'm really afraid of a pretty flower . . ."

He reached up to grab the fruit. A vine instantly shot out and coiled around the pair's feet.

The vines suddenly rose, moving like cranes as they lifted Manny and Diego above an enormous white blossom. There was an odd sucking sound, and then the huge petals stretched toward them.

"Oh boy . . ." Manny panicked as the flower slowly surrounded him and Diego. Within minutes, the petals had swallowed them both up to their shoulders. The two of them were pressed so close; they were nearly kissing each other.

Thwoop! A second later, the flower had completely encased them.

The others stood watching in horror.

"Stop eating our friends, plant!" Eddie yelled. Desperately, he and Crash charged at the flower.

Fwip! Fwip!

Vines shot from the ground in front of the flower, heading straight for the possums. Terrified, the two of them halted and then sprinted back in the other direction.

Ellie had seen enough. "That's it!" she declared. "I'm tearing that thing up from the roots."

A voice came from out of nowhere. "Do that and it'll clamp shut forever."

Ellie whirled around. It was Buck!

"Alright," he told her. "I'll have them out

before they're digested."

"*Digested?*" Manny echoed, poking his head out of the plant.

Inside the flower, a liquid began to rise.

Buck hacked open a stubby plant nearby. Sappy goop oozed out.

"They'll be nothing but bones in three minutes . . . maybe five for the fat one," Buck said.

"I'm not fat!" yelled Manny.

Ellie looked at Buck. "Hurry!" she yelled.

"It's time to get Buck Wild!" he declared.

Buck punched a few small blossoms out of his way and then jumped onto the petal of another plant. Vaulting into a somersault, he dived into the plant.

The juice had reached Manny and Diego's chins. Buck held his knife in his mouth and plunged to the bottom. Diego and Manny held their breath as the liquid rose past their mouths.

At the bottom, Buck pulled open a flap that covered the plant's blue and red stamens. He squinted and scratched his head—he had no idea which one to pull. He reached for the red one, sending menacing-looking bubbles rushing through the fluid.

Uh-oh, Buck thought. *Wrong one!* He worked frantically to tie the red stamen back together and then cut the blue one.

Ellie watched nervously. Suddenly, she saw the plant shudder and tighten.

What's happening? she thought in panic.

Then, one by one, the petals on the giant flower began to unfurl. Digestive juice splashed over the side.

Ellie stepped back as Manny and Diego

dropped down near her feet, covered in digestive goop and gasping for air. She rushed over to make sure they were okay.

"Barfed up by a plant!" Crash said.

"Awesome!" Eddie chimed in.

A few minutes later, Manny and Diego stood in front of the weasel, their fur matted and bedraggled. They looked down sheepishly.

"Go on," Ellie urged them. "Say it!"

Diego and Manny shuffled toward Buck.

"Uhh-uhh," Manny stammered. "Thank you for saving us."

"What he said," Diego put in.

Buck turned his head slightly, acknowledging their thanks.

Ellie rolled her eyes. "What they're trying to say is, would you please help us?"

Buck whipped around. He grabbed

Manny by the trunk and yanked him down to eye level.

"Alright," he snarled, "I'll help you. But I got rules. Rule number one: Always listen to Buck. Rule number two: Stay in the middle of the trail. Rule number three: He who has gas travels in the back of the pack."

Eddie slunk to the rear.

"Come on then. Chop chop!" Buck finished. With a flourish, he turned—and immediately crashed into a bush.

As Ellie and Diego followed, Manny leaped to Ellie's side to protect her.

"We should have our heads examined," Manny muttered.

Buck heard him. "That's rule number four!" he declared loudly.

CHAPTER TWELVE

Sid looked around desperately as the mother dinosaur stomped through a valley, carrying him and the three kids in her mouth.

The young dinosaurs whimpered in fear.

"Don't worry," he tried to comfort them. "Everything's okay. We're going to be fine."

Momma stopped in a clearing to let them down.

"See?" Sid said. "She's putting us—"

Before he could finish, Momma rose abruptly, still holding Sid.

He screamed. "Aaaagh! Nooo! I'm too young to be eaten!" He reached for a tree branch, trying to save himself.

Momma stopped, stretching Sid like a hammock.

"Please," Sid begged. "Don't do that!"

She continued to stretch him.

THWAP!

Sid suddenly snapped like a rubber band, flying right into a tree.

The dinosaur babies cowered behind a rock. Sid stood high in the tree while Momma loomed over him, an angry look in her eye.

"Listen," Sid said nervously. "Families can get complicated. Maybe we can work out something!"

CHOMP!

Momma lunged at the tree, snapping her jaws. Leaves flew everywhere as Sid scooted across a long tree bough.

"I could take the kids from Sunday to Tuesday," Sid tried again. "And you—"

It's a beautiful day on the tundra.

Scrat is still after that acorn,

as Diego looks out over the valley.

Manny and Ellie are expecting a baby.

Sid thinks he'll make a good-looking uncle . . .

a *clumsy*, good-looking uncle.

When the sloth finds three eggs underground,

he decides to become their parent.

Soon after, he is brought to
a strange, new jungle world

where dinosaurs rule . . .

and don't eat their vegetables!

Sid finds it hard to fit in here, too.

Meanwhile, Ellie wants to find Sid and bring him back home.

She leads the search party into the jungle after their missing friend.

Along the way, the gang meets a weasel named Buck who warns of great danger— and large dino teeth—ahead.

Will Manny and the gang ever find Sid?

CHOMP!

This time Momma devoured half the branch. By now, Sid hung from just a skinny twig.

"Maybe I could just take them on weekends?" he asked meekly.

Momma was furious. She bit into what was left of the tree. As Sid flew off, his feet got caught in a tangle of thick vines. The next thing he knew, he was hanging upside down by his ankle, dangling two inches above the ground.

Momma growled, advancing toward him.

He gulped. "If you eat me, it will send a bad message to our kids!"

She came closer, snapping her jaws. But just before she reached Sid, the three baby dinosaurs stepped between them. Baby Dinosaur One bared his teeth and let out a little growl.

Their mother looked at them in surprise. Then, to Sid's astonishment, she stepped backward.

Sid grinned. "Score one for the sloth!" he exclaimed. As he raised his arm in victory, he smacked himself right in the head.

Buck peeked through the thick foliage.

"So you're just living down here by your wits? All alone, with no responsibilities?" asked Diego.

"Yep. It's incredible," Buck replied. "No dependents, no limits—it's the greatest life a single guy could have."

Diego was impressed. "Did you hear that?" he asked Manny.

Manny nodded, watching Buck pick up a small rock and put it to his ear.

"Hello," said the weasel, as if the rock were a phone. He turned his back. "Look, I can't talk right now; I'm trying to recover a dead sloth. Yeah," he went on, "I love you, too."

Buck turned to face them again. "Okay, follow me," he said brightly.

Diego stared at him, incredulous.

"That's you in three weeks," Manny muttered into his friend's ear. "Totally nuts."

"So why do they call it the Chasm of Death?" asked Eddie.

Buck didn't answer. Instead, he reached into a tree. A hidden system of vines and pulleys raised into place, spanning the gap. A huge plate bone gondola dropped down in front of them.

"Madame . . ." Buck invited Ellie onto the contraption with an extended hand.

"Whoa! She's not doing that—" protested Manny.

"Bup-bup-bup-bup! Rule number one!" retorted Buck.

"Always listen to Buck!" said Ellie, as she walked past Manny.

Ellie climbed aboard and Buck clambered up to her shoulder.

"Now: eyes forward, back straight, and—oh yes—breathe in the toxic fumes and you'll probably die," remembered Buck.

"Toxic fumes?!" panicked Ellie.

"Wait!" ordered Manny.

But it was too late.

Buck wailed as he pulled a lever. "Geronimo!" The gondola zoomed over the chasm with Ellie and Buck, disappearing behind the cloud of green fumes.

"Ellie! You okay?" yelled Manny.

"You have to try this!" squealed Ellie.

"Alright! Now pile on everyone! Couldn't be easier!" encouraged Buck.

CHAPTER THIRTEEN

The young dinos whimpered hungrily as they stood around a flat rock, waiting to eat.

Sid arrived with an armful of vegetables and tossed them down. "Okay, here you go, guys. Eat! Eat!"

The kids sniffed the food and then turned away in disgust.

"What?" Sid stared at them. "You're not going to eat your vegetables? How are you ever going to become big strong dinosaurs?"

Just then, Momma dropped an archaeopteryx, a dinosaur bird, in front of the kids.

They looked at her, clueless. She motioned toward the bird, telling them to eat it.

"No way!" Sid said, blocking the bird. "I've raised them to be vegetarians—not meat eaters. It's a much healthier lifestyle," he went on. "Look at me. I have the pelt of a much younger sloth."

Ignoring Sid, the mother pushed the bird toward the hungry kids.

Sid could see the dinosaurs eyeing the archaeopteryx, considering it. "No, no, no!" he told them. "That's not for us, kids. It's way too feathery and fleshy and—"

Suddenly, the meal looked up at him!

"And alive!" he finished.

Sid jumped back. The bird, equally terrified, flopped after him. It flapped a few feet in the air like a chicken and then landed in his arms. There was a pleading look in its eyes.

Sid turned to Momma and the kids. "No! We do not eat live animals. Period!" he told them.

He carried the bird to the edge of the cliff. "Now go. Fly and be free!"

He tossed the bird off the cliff, not realizing that it didn't know how to fly. The flightless bird plummeted like a stone—until a hungry pterodactyl snatched it in midair and gulped it down in one bite.

Momma snorted angrily and turned back to the bushes.

"Hey!" Sid called after her. "Where are you going? No wonder you're single. You can't resolve conflicts like this!"

Momma responded by dropping an animal carcass in front of her young. She glared at Sid.

"Oh, come on," he complained. "Am

I talking to myself here? I say, 'They're vegetarian.' You say, 'Grrrr.' I say, 'Can we talk about this?' And you say 'Grrr' again. I don't call that communication!"

"Grrr," answered the dinosaur.

"That's your answer to everything!" Sid declared in frustration.

A bone rolled in front of him. He and Momma turned to look at the kids—and saw that the carcass was now a pile of bones. The dinos let out a series of burps, looking plump and satisfied.

Sid was about to scold them when a ferocious growl echoed around them.

Momma swiftly gathered up the kids and began to hurry away. The kids whimpered, though, reaching for Sid.

Another growl came, this time followed by thundering footsteps, rapidly drawing nearer.

With a sigh, Momma reached down and scooped up Sid.

Minutes later, a giant shadow spilled over the rock where they had just been. The creature bent down and sniffed the area hungrily.

CHAPTER FOURTEEN

That night, Crash and Eddie sat around a glowing lava pit with Buck, hanging on his every word while he told them the story of how he'd lost one eye.

"There I was," Buck went on, "my back against the wall, perched on the razor's edge of destiny, with no way out. I was staring into the heart of darkness—"

"What happened next?" Eddie asked eagerly.

"I thought I'd gotten away from Rudy when the next thing I knew, he snatched me up in his enormous jaws!"

Crash gasped. "Were you killed?" he asked.

Buck gave him a look. "Uh, no."

Even Manny found himself creeping closer to the fire so he could hear the rest of the story.

"Never had I felt more alive than when I was so close to death," Buck went on. "Just before Rudy could suck me down his gullet, I grabbed hold of that pink fleshy thing that dangles in the back of the throat—"

"Ew! Gross!" the possums burst out.

"I hung on to that sucker," Buck went on, "and I swung back and forth, back and forth until finally I let go and shot right out of his mouth. I may have lost my eye that day," he added, "but I got this."

Eddie gasped as Buck whipped out a razor-sharp weapon. "Rudy's tooth!"

The possums were totally impressed.

"You are Super-Weasel!" Eddie said.

"Ultra-Weasel!" Crash said.

"Diesel-Weasel!" Diego put in.

Manny gave him a look.

"What?" Diego said with a shrug. "He is."

Buck placed the sheath over his knife, Rudy's tooth. "Yes, I am," he agreed. "Now let me tell you another story, about the time I—"

"Whoa, whoa," Manny cut in. "That's enough fairy tales for one night."

Buck looked at him. "You don't believe me?"

"Let's just say I believe that you believe it," Manny retorted. "Isn't that enough?"

"It sure is," Buck replied.

"Good," Manny answered. "Let's get some sleep. Come on, Ellie," he added, leading her away.

"You guys get some shut-eye," Buck told everyone. "I'll keep watch."

The possums shook their heads.

"Don't worry, Buck," Eddie said. "We've got this. Nighttime is possum time!"

"We own the night, baby!" echoed Crash.

Minutes later, the campsite was quiet. Manny, Ellie, and Diego were sound asleep—and so were Crash and Eddie. While the possums snored loudly, Buck remained wide-awake, listening for Rudy and keeping watch over all of them.

Momma lifted the little dinosaurs one at a time and placed them in the nest she'd built on a cliff high above the ground.

Sid scrambled after them, but his foot kept slipping, sending him tumbling downward.

Finally, he gave up. "Sleep well, kids," he yelled up to them. "We have a busy day tomorrow, foraging, hunting . . . and . . . missing my friends," he added sadly. He paused for a second, thinking about Manny and Ellie and the others and remembering that terrible scene in Manny's playground. "I miss them, but they probably don't miss me at all," he murmured.

Sid sighed and spread out a giant plant frond to make a bed for himself. Then, to his surprise, Momma leaned down and lifted him by the collar.

"Whoa!" he cried nervously.

Momma gently put him down in the nest, right beside the kids.

Sid was touched. "You're a real softie, you know that?"

Momma snorted, annoyed, but Sid could see that she was smiling a little. As he curled up with the kids, Momma turned around. Then she stared alertly out at the jungle, guarding her young with her life.

Ellie's eyes blinked open. "Manny?" she called.

Looking around, she saw that the campground was empty. "Crash? Eddie?"

An ominous sound came from the jungle. Ellie turned, startled. Then she began walking toward the sound. "Manny?"

Two yellow eyes suddenly blinked open! And then . . . a terrifying pair of jaws sprung out of the darkness!

Gasping, Manny woke up. When he looked around the campsite, he saw Ellie nearby, still sleeping peacefully.

It was a dream, just a dream, he told himself. Still, he went over to check on her.

"Manny?" Ellie said groggily. "Are you okay?"

"I'm sorry," Manny blurted out. "I just wanted to keep you safe, and now you're in the most dangerous place in the world!"

"This isn't your fault," Ellie told him firmly. "Life happens. You've just got to roll with it."

Manny shook his head. "If I'd been a better friend to Sid, we wouldn't be here," he said.

"*Better friend?*" a voice echoed. "Are you plucking my whiskers?"

Buck dropped down in front of them on a vine. "You risked your life, your mate, and your baby to save your buddy," he told Manny. "You may not be the best husband or father, but you're a darned good friend."

Manny sighed, not knowing what to say. He was still filled with doubts—would they ever see Sid again?

CHAPTER
FIFTEEN

An eerie morning mist swirled through the thick grass as Buck led the way into a clearing.

"Everybody stop!" he cried.

They all stopped in their tracks. Buck's eyes darted all around, finally landing on a large flat rock. "I smell something," he announced, picking up a tuft of fur.

He sniffed it and then recoiled. "It smells like a buzzard's butt fell off and then got sprayed by a bunch of skunks!"

Diego beamed. "That's Sid!"

"He's alive!" Ellie cried.

"We have ourselves a crime scene." Buck pointed to various clues. "Tufts of

fur. Half-eaten carcass. Hunk of broccoli."
He whirled around. "Here's what I think
happened: Dinosaur attacked Sid. Sid
fought back with piece of broccoli, leaving
dinosaur a vegetable."

Diego stared at him. "Are you nuts? Sid's
not violent. Or coordinated," he added.

"Yeah," Manny put in. "And where's the
dinosaur?"

"All right, good points," Buck admitted.
"Theory two: Sid's eating broccoli. Dinosaur
eats Sid. Dinosaur steps on broccoli, leaving
broccoli a vegetable."

"Buck, when exactly did you lose your
mind?" Diego asked.

"Three months ago," Buck replied.
"I woke up one morning married to a
pineapple. An ugly pineapple," he added
with a sigh. "But I loved her."

Diego's stomach lurched. Ahead was

a tree that was deeply gouged with claw marks. "What about this?" he asked, showing Buck.

The weasel blinked. "Well, your friend might be alive, but not for long. Rudy's on their tail."

The group trudged on to the plains of woe, a dusty collection of parched plates. Ellie felt herself lagging behind as they continued tracking Sid and the dinosaurs. Manny dropped back, worried about her.

"Ellie," he started to say. "Are you—"

"I'm fine," she cut him off.

Just then, the plates below Ellie began to crack and crumble.

"Ellie!" yelped Manny.

Crash! Crack!

At the last moment, Ellie leaped onto a safe, protected ledge. The rest of the group ran, leaped, and dodged as the entire environment collapsed around them.

The dust settled on the trail, strewn with debris. Buck dusted off his fur. A little bit woozy, the possums, Manny, and Diego regrouped.

"Where's Ellie?" cried Manny.

"It's okay!" Ellie yelled, from her ledge. "I'm over here."

"Hang on! We'll be right there!" reassured Manny as the group followed Ellie's voice.

CHAPTER SIXTEEN

"**W**ait! Time out!" Sid yelled. He struggled to keep up with the baby dinosaurs as they galloped ahead of him, chasing an archaeopteryx.

"*Sheesh!*" Sid complained. "You guys are getting too fast." He stopped to catch his breath, looking around. The jungle seemed dark and menacing. Surly-looking dinosaurs passed by, glaring at him.

"It's not so bad down here," Sid tried to tell himself. "There's nice weather, friendly neighbors . . ."

Just then a shadow fell on the sloth. Hot breath ruffled his fur. Sid turned to see . . . Rudy.

"Oh boy." Sid gulped.

* * *

Moving carefully, the group of mammals mounted a jumble of saucerlike rock platforms that led up to a ledge.

ROAR!

A terrifying growl echoed all around them.

Buck recognized it at once. "Rudy!" he cried.

A high-pitched scream followed.

Buck frowned. "I never heard that kind of dino before," he said.

But Manny recognized the cry immediately. "That's Sid!" he exclaimed.

"They must be over by Lava Falls," said Buck. "We'll have to move fast."

"Manny! The baby's coming!" Ellie called suddenly.

"Just sit tight! We're on our way!" Manny answered.

Buck took charge. "There's only one

thing to do." He turned to Crash and Eddie. "Possums, you're with me. Manny, you take care of Ellie until we get back."

"What?" Manny shook his head. "No! No! You can't leave now. She's off the trail! What about rule number two?"

"Rule number five says you can ignore rule number two if there's a female involved, or possibly a cute dog. . . ." Buck's voice trailed off. "You know, I just make up these rules as I go along."

"Yeah, but—" Manny stammered. "You have to—"

Diego stepped up. "It's all right, Manny," he said. "I've got your back."

"Now you're talking," Buck said with a nod. "Come on," he told the possums. "Let's go."

They raced over to Manny. "Take care of her," said Crash.

Manny stood there numbly, not knowing to do.

"We've got to move," Diego told him.

Manny finally nodded, and they continued climbing the saucer-shaped rocks.

Ellie sat on a ledge as terrible pains shuddered through her. "It's okay. Daddy's coming," she murmured.

In the distance, a guanlong dinosaur popped out from under a large, flat rock. He looked over at Ellie's perch, hissing loudly and flashing his razor-sharp claws. From behind him, more guanlongs appeared. Silently, they began creeping toward her.

CHAPTER SEVENTEEN

Buck stood with the possums on top of a cliff. He dropped down in front of them. "Boys! Are you ready for adventure?"

"Yes, sir!" Crash and Eddie replied.

"For danger?" Buck asked.

"Yes, sir!"

"For death?" Buck demanded.

Crash and Eddie looked at each other. "Can you repeat the question?" asked Crash.

"JUMP!" Buck cried. At that, he leaped off the cliff nearby, yanking the possums with him. Eddie and Crash screamed in terror as they plunged downward.

In the nick of time they landed on the back of a giant pterodactyl. The creature shook its tail, sending them flying.

In midair, Buck managed to lasso the pterodactyl and rein it in. He spun the bird around, catching Eddie and Crash. While Buck sat on its neck, steering the large bird, the possums clung desperately to its back.

"Uh, Buck?" Crash asked, terrified. "Have you ever flown one of these before?"

"It's my first time actually!" Buck said, spurring on the bird. "Yee-haw!" he cried, like a cowboy.

"There she is!" cried Diego.

As Manny and Diego turned a corner, they spotted Ellie hunched on a remote alcove.

"Ellie!" cried Manny.

"Manny!" she yelled back.

Hiss!

Manny and Diego turned to see a

horde of guanlongs approaching Ellie from another direction.

"I need to get to her," Manny said urgently.

But as he started toward the next rock platform, Diego stopped him. "Manny, you hold back the dinosaurs. I can get to Ellie faster. You have to trust me!" he added.

Manny glanced at the approaching attackers, his heart filled with dread. Then he looked back at Ellie, who was watching them nervously and calling his name. He desperately wanted to go to her, but he knew Diego was right.

He turned back to his friend and they locked eyes. "Let's do it," he said.

Manny and Diego sprang into action. Diego raced toward Ellie, leaping across the saucer-shaped rocks with lightning speed. Meanwhile, Manny hurtled toward the attacking dinosaurs. The guanlongs surrounded him, eyeing him menacingly.

Diego reached Ellie, breathing hard. "Are you all right?" he asked her.

"Am I all right?" she shot back. "Do you know anything about childbirth?"

"No, not really," Diego admitted. "But Manny's coming."

Ellie let out a sharp cry.

"It's just a contraction," Diego told her. "You're going to be fine."

"No!" Ellie shook her head and pointed. A guanlong was climbing toward them.

Diego tackled it and then knocked back another. Suddenly, his eyes went wide: An entire herd of guanlongs was scaling the cliff, headed right for him!

Manny knocked away guanlongs. They kept coming, swarming out of a nest high in the rocks.

Manny ran over and smashed a rock against the hole, trying to hold the dinosaurs back.

Above, Ellie's pains were coming faster and faster.

"Don't worry about a thing. It's all under control," Diego coached her. "Just stay calm. Deep breaths."

He punched away one more guanlong. Another one grabbed Diego's back paw, dragging him off the edge.

"Just breathe!" he yelled to Ellie, as the guanlong pulled him along.

"Diego!" Ellie cried.

The saber-toothed tiger popped his head over the ledge, coaching her as he continued to fight off the attacking dinosaurs. "That's fine! You're doing great!"

Meanwhile, Manny struggled to hold the rock against the mob of guanlongs. Looking around, he spotted a tree holding up a pile of rocks. He smashed into its trunk, causing an avalanche. The falling rocks forced the guanlongs to retreat into the hole—and then the rocks sealed the opening!

A guanlong's tail smacked Diego back onto the ledge with Ellie. He tumbled and landed right in front of her.

"Diego?" she said. "I'm scared."

Diego nodded, trying to swallow his own fear. Gently, he wiped her brow with water from a nearby spring.

"Don't worry," he said. "I'm right here. Everything will be fine."

"Can I hold your paw?" she asked.

"Of course," he answered.

She wrapped her trunk around his paw, squeezing so tightly that Diego dropped to his knees in pain.

CHAPTER
EIGHTEEN

Aboard the pterodactyl, Buck struggled to steer. He narrowly missed the craggy cliffs and tall dinosaurs below.

"He's right there!" Crash shouted suddenly, pointing to a figure standing on a rock in the lava river.

Buck gripped the reins. "Roger!" he said. "I see him."

Buck guided the pterodactyl toward Sid. Eddie looked back—there was a flock of pterodactyls on their tail, eyeing the possums hungrily!

"Uh, Buck?!" Eddie said.

Buck performed a series of dazzling maneuvers to escape their pursuers, diving under and over the necks of tall brontosauruses. Just when he thought he'd lost the pterodactyls, they flew right into an oncoming flock!

By now Buck was an ace flier. He deftly maneuvered around the pterodactyls.

He swerved toward a tree. "Grab that ammo!" he shouted to the possums.

Crash and Eddie grabbed bunches of fruit as they flew past the tree. Then Eddie loaded fruit onto Crash's tail as if were a bow.

"Ready?" Eddie asked.

"FIRE!" Crash shouted back.

Eddie hit one bird in the eye, making it sputter and then fly out of control. Together they took down one bird after another.

"Let's get our sloth!" Buck shouted.

Wham!

A pterodactyl swooped in, taking out

Buck. Crash and Eddie were left holding the reins, desperately trying to control their bird-plane.

Buck hung onto the tail of one pterodactyl as other, attacking pterodactyls snapped at him from behind.

Crash and Eddie looked up. To their horror, they were headed right toward Lava Falls! They yanked on the reins with all their might, but they couldn't control their bird-plane!

Buck saw what was happening. He swung up onto one bird's wing and then slid down the back of another, launching himself onto the back of the first pterodactyl. Just as they were about to fly straight into the falls, Buck grabbed the reins and pulled hard. The pterodactyl instantly went into a vertical climb, just inches from the sizzling lava.

Above, Sid was desperately trying to escape the waterfall of lava, too. He jumped from rock to rock until . . . there were no more rocks!

He gulped as the current of lava pulled him over the falls, and then . . .

Thwwoomp!

The pterodactyl rocketed past and scooped him up. He dangled from the bottom of the bird.

"Woo-hoo!" cried Eddie and Crash triumphantly.

Sid still didn't realize he'd been rescued. "Help!" screamed the sloth. "Momma! Save me from this bird!"

"No, Sid!" Crash and Eddie yelled at him. "It's us! You're okay!"

Sid blinked in surprise. "The whole gang? For me?"

The pterodactyl continued its vertical

climb. It soared higher and higher, all the way to the ice ceiling. Suddenly, it dived down, right near Momma and the kids.

When Momma spotted Sid, still dangling from the bird, she let out a shriek and charged after them. Her young followed closely behind.

"Wait—my kids!" Sid cried. "I have to say good-bye!"

Diego and Ellie lay side by side. While Ellie fought through birthing pains, Diego fought back attacking dinosaurs. He pushed a log hard, sending it rolling off the cliff and knocking dinosaurs over the side.

Diego held Ellie's trunk. "Breathe," he coached her. "You can do this, Ellie!"

As Manny made his way up the rocky cliff, he heard Ellie cry in pain. He picked up his pace.

A guanlong suddenly leaped at Diego from out of nowhere. Just as it was about to sink in its teeth, the creature was yanked backward.

"Manny!" Diego cried. His friend had made it!

Manny tossed the guanlong off the side of the cliff. As he whirled around, he heard a baby cry.

Manny took a deep breath and then moved toward Ellie, his eyes landing on an adorable baby mammoth.

Manny choked up. Everything he'd been waiting for and hoping for was right here. Tears filled his eyes as Ellie met his gaze. She smiled, looking very, very tired.

Manny reached down and gently stroked the baby with his trunk. Ellie reached over with her trunk to clasp Manny's.

"She's perfect. I think we should call her

Ellie. Little Ellie," Manny told her.

"I've got a better name . . . Peaches," Ellie said.

"Peaches?" asked Manny.

"Why not? She's sweet and round and covered with fuzz," responded Ellie.

Ellie looked up and saw Diego wiping away a tear. "I saw that, tough guy," she teased him.

"No, no," Diego lied. "That wasn't what you think. The last dino caught my eye with a claw and . . ."

His friends looked at him, grinning.

"All right, all right," the saber admitted a second later. "I'm not made of stone."

Manny smiled. He was about to say more when someone shouted, "Incoming!"

Manny turned to see a pterodactyl flying right at them. Sid dangled from its talons, a goofy grin plastered on his face.

The pterodactyl released the sloth. He hit the ground and rolled toward the baby.

"It's a girl!" Sid cried. "Hi, sweetheart! It's Uncle Sid. Oh, you're so beautiful!" he gushed. "She looks just like her mother," he told Manny. "Thank goodness for that. I mean, no offense, Manny. You're beautiful on the inside."

Manny ruffled Sid's fur affectionately, glad to see his friend back in one piece.

Eddie and Crash dropped down, taking in the scene.

"I promised myself I wouldn't cry," Eddie said, gulping.

"I didn't," Crash said, and then he burst into tears.

"Look, Peaches, all of our friends are here," said Ellie.

"We wouldn't have it any other way," said Manny.

CHAPTER NINETEEN

Buck let out a sigh as he watched the happy reunion. Then he glanced up at the darkening sky. "This is it, mammals," he said, "right where you started. This was fun. We could make it a regular thing—"

"I don't know about that," said Ellie.

"We couldn't have done it without you," Manny thanked Buck.

Suddenly, red eyes opened in the darkness of the cave behind Buck.

Manny stared in disbelief as the creature's massive, battled-scarred head blotted out the sun. The dinosaur bared his teeth, showing a missing one in front.

Rudy! Manny realized. He was much

bigger and meaner-looking than Manny had ever imagined. Ellie, Peaches, and the possums ran for safety.

"Run!" Buck cried. The weasel ran forward and diverted Rudy's attention. He pulled out his knife, licked his scar, and led Rudy away from the others. He ran across tree tops and smashed through the canopy like a whale breaching.

Thinking fast, he spotted something in the rocks nearby. "Shoo! Shoo!" he cried.

A flock of giant moths lifted into flight. They swarmed around Rudy in a cloud.

The dinosaur staggered backward, swatting away the moths. Buck seized the moment to slip from Rudy's claw, dropping to the ground.

The moths flew off. Buck took out his knife, squinting at the dinosaur.

Rudy squinted right back, his tongue

slithering around the gap in his teeth. He leaned in, about to attack, when an angry shriek filled the air. Rudy whirled around, but it was too late. Momma was already knocking him forward with a headbutt to his back.

Rudy squawked as he slammed into a stone tower. Rocks showered down everywhere.

"Way to go, *Mom-zilla!*" cried Sid.

Momma snorted with satisfaction while the baby dinosaurs stood under her belly, imitating her ferocious stance.

Rudy climbed to his feet and began to approach Momma for another face-off. Sid and the kids took cover behind a rock while Buck glanced around, trying to locate his weapons.

The two dinosaurs faced each other, clawing, snapping, and whipping each other with their tails. Buck grabbed his knife and then leaped onto a vine. He swung toward Rudy, a determined look on his face.

Bam!

Buck slammed into Momma instead, as she stepped in front of him.

Rudy swiped Momma hard, and she went down. He loomed over her, about to finish her off. Suddenly, the baby dinosaurs raced over, attacking Rudy's feet and knocking him to the ground!

Buck raced over to lasso the big creature's snout.

Rudy climbed to his feet again, thrashing his head and whipping Buck through the air. Momma came to in time to see Rudy kicking her babies off him.

She snarled and then charged, furiously knocking Rudy through a rock pillar—and right over the edge of a deep crevasse!

The great beast tumbled down into the void, shrieking loudly all the way.

CHAPTER
TWENTY

Momma let out a victory roar. The baby dinos did the same thing, rushing over to her.

The kids nuzzled her closely, too. Sid watched, moved by the scene. *They love her,* he realized. *She's their mother, and they love her.*

"You're where you belong now," he told them softly. "And I'm sure you'll grow up to be giant horrifying dinosaurs, just like your mother."

He looked up at Momma, choked up. "Take good care of our kids, okay?"

Momma stepped toward Sid and gently licked his hair into a Mohawk. Then she threw back her head and let out a sad roar, her way of saying good-bye.

Sid did the same thing, only his roar sounded more like someone gargling. He sighed, watching his family go.

Manny and Diego came up behind him.

"You were a good parent, Sid," Manny put in, meaning it.

"Thanks," Sid replied. He waited for a second and then asked, "So, can I babysit for you?"

Manny shook his head. "Not a chance."

"I work cheap," Sid tried again.

"All right," Manny said, "I'll think about it." He turned to Diego and whispered, "Never happen."

Buck stood nearby, staring numbly into the crevasse where Rudy had fallen.

"Are you okay?" Diego asked him.

Buck nodded. "I can't believe he's gone, that's all." He looked at Diego. "Now what am I supposed to do?"

"That's easy!" Ellie chimed in. "Come with us!"

Buck stared at her. "You mean, up there?"

"We can't leave you behind," Manny said, with a smile.

"Wow . . ." Buck stared at them, touched and surprised by the invitation. "I've been down here for so long, I've never really considered going back. I'm not sure if I fit in up there anymore."

"So?" Diego said. "Look at us. Do we look like a normal herd to you?"

Buck stood, thinking for a moment. His new friends definitely did not look like a normal herd.

CHAPTER
TWENTY-ONE

Rock and dirt rained down from the ceiling of the cavern as the gang continued on their way back home to the Ice Age. They were almost there now.

Buck stopped at the base of the steps, speaking into a rock.

"I told you not to fall in love with me," he murmured. "We can still be friends. And if you're ever in the Ice Age, look me up!"

The others waited for him.

"You coming, Buck?" called Eddie.

"Right behind you," answered the weasel.

One by one, the friends moved through

the tunnel that led back home.

"We're almost out!" Sid said.

Diego crossed, and then it was Buck's turn. With boulders dropping down all around him, he took one last look back. He stopped to listen for something, but it didn't come.

"So long, Rudy," the weasel said sadly. With a sigh, he took out his knife and drove it into the ground. He started up the last steps when there was a thunderous roar in the distance.

Buck stopped and broke into an ecstatic grin. *Rudy!*

"He's back!" he cried.

"Buck!" Diego called.

"I . . . ," Buck hesitated, and then gestured toward the sound. He looked up at Diego. "I've got to . . ."

Diego nodded. "I understand," he said.

"Besides, this world should really stay down here," he added. He reached for his knife and quickly swiped it through the key joints of the bridge. Immediately, it began to buckle and groan.

Buck turned to Diego and gave a final salute. "Take care of them, tiger!"

Diego returned the salute. "Always listen to Buck," he replied.

Buck smiled as the bridge crumbled underneath him in a cloud of dust. Then he grabbed onto a vine and swung back toward his home.

"Woo-hoo!" Diego heard him whoop.

As the baby mammoth scrambled out of the hole, she blinked in the bright sunlight.

"We made it!" Eddie cried. He bent down and kissed the ice, his lips getting stuck to the frozen surface.

Manny had just climbed out when there was a loud *kaboom!*

Behind him the cavern collapsed, a cloud of debris billowing out from the hole.

"Is everybody okay?" Manny called.

Eddie looked around. "Where are Buck and Diego?" he asked in alarm.

Diego raced out of the dust. "I'm right here," he said, "and Buck is where he wants to be." Diego then realized he felt the exact same way.

"Do you think he's okay?" Crash asked anxiously.

"Are you kidding?" said Diego with a grin. "It's *Rudy* I'm worried about!"

Ellie put Peaches down on the ice. The baby mammoth started to slide, but Ellie came to her rescue.

Manny turned to Diego. "I know this

'baby makes three' thing isn't for you, but—"

"I'm not leaving, buddy," Diego cut him off. "Life of adventure?" He smiled widely. "It's right here."

"But I've got a whole speech ready for you," Manny protested. "I was about to show you that I'm strong—and sensitive, not to mention noble, yet caring."

In reply, Diego punched Manny on his shoulder.

"Ow!" said Manny. Then he grinned. "Thanks."

Baby Peaches looked all around, amazed at the new white world surrounding her. She giggled and reached out with her trunk to catch some of the tiny snowflakes falling from the sky.

"Welcome to the Ice Age, Peaches," Ellie said, nuzzling her baby girl. She beamed with happiness as she gazed at the familiar frozen landscape and then at the members of her family—her own special herd. "We finally made it home!"